Samuel French Acting Edition

The Cake

by Bekah Brunstetter

SAMUELFRENCH.COM   SAMUELFRENCH.CO.UK

FOR PRODUCTION ENQUIRIES

UNITED STATES AND CANADA
Info@SamuelFrench.com
1-866-598-8449

UNITED KINGDOM AND EUROPE
Plays@SamuelFrench.co.uk
020-7255-4302

Each title is subject to availability from Samuel French, depending upon country of performance. Please be aware that *THE CAKE* may not be licensed by Samuel French in your territory. Professional and amateur producers should contact the nearest Samuel French office or licensing partner to verify availability.

MUSIC USE NOTE

Licensees are solely responsible for obtaining formal written permission from copyright owners to use copyrighted music in the performance of this play and are strongly cautioned to do so. If no such permission is obtained by the licensee, then the licensee must use only original music that the licensee owns and controls. Licensees are solely responsible and liable for all music clearances and shall indemnify the copyright owners of the play(s) and their licensing agent, Samuel French, against any costs, expenses, losses and liabilities arising from the use of music by licensees. Please contact the appropriate music licensing authority in your territory for the rights to any incidental music.

IMPORTANT BILLING AND CREDIT REQUIREMENTS

If you have obtained performance rights to this title, please refer to your licensing agreement for important billing and credit requirements.

THE CAKE was first produced by the Echo Theater Company (Artistic Director, Chris Fields; Producing Director, Jesse Cannady) in Los Angeles on June 28, 2017. The performance was directed by Jennifer Chambers, with sets by Pete Hickok, costumes by Elena Flores, and sound design by Jeff Gardner. The production stage manager was Natalie Figaredo. The cast was as follows:

DELLA	Debra Jo Rupp
TIM	Joe Hart
JEN	Shannon Lucio
MACY	Carolyn Ratteray
GEORGE	Morrison Keddie

THE CAKE was originally produced in New York City by the Manhattan Theatre Club (Artistic Director, Lynne Meadow; Executive Producer, Barry Grove) on February 12, 2019. The performance was directed by Lynne Meadow, with scenic design by John Lee Beatty, costume design by Tom Broecker, lighting design by Philip S. Rosenberg, and original music & sound design by John Gromada. The production stage manager was Stephen Ravet. The cast was as follows:

DELLA	Debra Jo Rupp
TIM	Dan Daily
JEN	Genevieve Angelson
MACY	Marinda Anderson

CHARACTERS

DELLA – forties/fifties, pleasant, round, with a mass of big, curly hair

TIM – forties/fifties, her husband, a good ol' boy

JEN – early thirties, with a wedding binder, has dreamt of her wedding day her whole life

MACY – early thirties, Jen's reluctant fiancée, African American

SETTING

North Carolina
A Bakery; A Home

TIME

Now

Scene One

DELLA *ices a cake with great concentration.*

The attention to detail is absurd. It is a glorious cake.

Darkness all around her. It's just her and this cake.

This is **DELLA** *on her throne, this is her with her bitch, this is her pulling the sword from the stone, this is her lovemaking, her second coming.*

A few moments of just this woman and this cake.

And then:

DELLA. See, what you *have* to do is really, *truly* follow the directions. That's what people don't understand. People watch the baking shows and they say to themselves: "I can do that. I am gonna make a cake from scratch. I am going to prove to myself that I am a person who is capable of such a thing." So they go out and they get all of the ingredients, bring 'em all home, set 'em on the counter.

First mistake they make: *Skimpin'*. Skimpin' on milk, skimpin' on butter, they try and use tofu butter or whatever, milk made outta *nuts*, what *is* this world? You gotta get the *real* stuff. And I don't mean that organic this or that stuff. I don't care whether or not your eggs were ever caged, whether they ever went to the movies, I'm talking about the FAT, buddy, full fat, you *gotta*. Why go to Rome if you're not gonna eat the pasta, why go to France if you're not gonna eat the baguettes?

Second mistake – they read in the cookbook: "Whisk the wet ingredients together for three minutes, then fold in the dry ingredients in quarter parts." And they think to themselves: "I don't really have to do all that, do I? That's just a suggestion. I can just mix it all together, pop it in a ungreased pan at 350, hope for the best." Well I say to those people: "You are *wrong*." If you're not gonna give your time and your worship to directions that have been crafted by trial and error, you might as well do a darn cake from a box, which tastes like Scotch tape dipped in Splenda if you're asking. If you're gonna do it from scratch, you gotta Follow. The. Directions.

> *She smooths the side of the cake with her butter knife. It's meditative.*

That's the only way you'll get that taste. It's the taste of time and obedience. All the scientists in the world could sit in a lab for eternity and never recreate it. So if you want results – if you want to make a cake that you could take a nap in, that you want to crawl inside of, that you would die for –

> *She starts to lose herself inside of something so beautiful she could come or cry.*

You must – follow – the directions.

> *Suddenly, the aggressive ding of an oven.*
>
> *Lights pop to include a bakery. It's charming, quaint, where your mom gets your birthday cake. There's a display case with cakes for all occasions, cuddled by cupcakes and muffins and blondies and brownies and donuts and sweet bread of every kind. Breathe in. Do it. Let yourself go there, fatty, don't hold back.*
>
> *Remember butter? Remember fat?*
>
> **DELLA** *stands behind the counter. She is suddenly and acutely aware of* **MACY**: *highly intelligent, wry, blunt, a beautiful tomboyishness to her.*

MACY is looking at **DELLA** *a bit wide-eyed, processing everything she just heard. She is delighted by her, she is processing her.*

So that's how I make them! So.

Sorry. Sometimes when I talk about my cakes I think I leave my body! I guess that was a long answer to your question.

MACY. Hey, no worries, I asked!

MACY *then spots an elaborate cake on the counter that looks more like a sculpture or prize than anything one might eat.*

What's that one for? It's very elaborate!

DELLA. Oh! It's a Noah's Ark Cake! It's for a baptism for my goddaughter. It's on Sunday.

She's not my goddaughter but she practically is. I'm her honorary godmother, is the technical arrangement, because her aunt made a real stink. "Blood relative." So.

It took me days to get the little critters! I made the little critters outta marzipan! See?

You got your elephants, you got your orangutans, you got your giraffes –

MACY *looks close. Little critters! Like Noah's Ark!*

MACY. *(Can't help herself.)* Where're the dinosaurs?

DELLA. Oh, I didn't have room for them. But they were on the ark, too.

MACY. Oh, okay! Right on.

DELLA. Are you a baker, Do you like to bake?

MACY. Oh God, no. I do *not* have the patience. Or the counter space.

*(**MACY** continues to take in the bakery. **DELLA** starts to feel self-conscious.)*

DELLA. ...First time to North Carolina?

MACY. I drove through it once, in high school, on the way down to Florida.

DELLA. Aww, for Disney World?!

MACY. Actually, it was for a national debate competition.

DELLA. Now, see, I just do not see the point of those, how is *arguing* a skill?

> **MACY** *now feels insulted.*

> **DELLA** *sees this.*

...But that musta been fun for you!

MACY. It was. I got second place.

DELLA. Well hey, look at you!

It really is a wonderful place to live. Beautiful food, beautiful people – oh! There's a vegetarian restaurant downtown! I believe it is called Asparagus! No, wait. Asparagus closed. It was disgusting!

> **DELLA** *laughs.*

> **MACY** *smiles.*

MACY. So what're your feelings on all the research about sugar, its addictive qualities, all that?

> **DELLA** *just looks at her blankly.*

DELLA. Hmm?

MACY. Apparently it's more addictive than cocaine. But it's in all of our foods, and so basically there's a new generation of young Americans who are practically *born* with diabetes, because when the food distributors decided that fat was bad for us, they started to load everything with sugar instead, to give it flavor, as we are humans, and we want to taste nice things, right?

DELLA. *(Trying to keep up.)* Yes! We do.

MACY. But REAL food has no taste these days. See, if I gave you a bowl of raspberries and a bag of Cool Ranch Doritos right now, you would / find that –

DELLA. Doritos!

MACY. Exactly! And so in forty years we're going to have a bunch of people who can't provide for themselves, they'll be so fat they can't leave their houses and so basically we'll be supporting them with our taxes, those of us who aren't dead from cancer, from, you know, basically everything else.

>*Beat.*

DELLA. Oh, okay! Well. Everything in moderation, my mother always said. And also I think Jackie O. I like to think that people should be able to control themselves. I can control myself.

I mean of course it's bad, in a way. Cut me open I'm sure I'm full'a jelly beans. But I get my meat and my potatas, too. I balance it out. And hey, you only live once and then it's off to eternity!

>**MACY** *just smiles. Gets out a journal. Starts to write.* **DELLA** *clocks this.*

Is this – so is this because of the show?

MACY. The –?

DELLA. *The Big American Bake-Off*!

MACY. I don't –?

DELLA. I'm about to be a contestant on *The Big American Bake-Off*! I thought maybe that's why / you're here.

MACY. Big American?

DELLA. Bake-Off!

>*(Off* **MACY***'s blank look.)* It's Tuesday nights on CBS.

MACY. Uh-huh.

DELLA. It's the top watched baking show in the country. I'm not bragging, but it's quite competitive to get picked. They have you do some videos to show your personality and you send those in with your recipes. I got my hair done and everything. Such a mess, all this hair. I have a feeling I could take it all the way, as long as I stick to the classics! That's how people get themselves kicked off. Tryin' too hard to be original. Cardamom kiwi this or that.

MACY. So it's a reality –?

DELLA. Baking competition. Each week you get three things to bake, and each week somebody gets kicked off. The winner gets twenty thousand dollars and a really big biscuit which is what they call cookies in England. I have watched every second of the British version. It's my sports. One guy made a lion outta bread. It was ABSURDITY. And then – there is *George*.

MACY. George – is –?

DELLA. He is one of the judges. And he is *so* handsome. I'm a married woman, but I can say that.

He's got a voice like a king. He speaks and it's true.

> *Suddenly stage lights are on her. She is exposed.*
>
> *The* **VOICE** *of a British judge.*

VOICE. Welcome back to *The Big American Bake-Off*! Thousands applied to the show, and only twelve have been selected to see WHO will be the BEST AMERICAN BAKER!

Della, lovely to have you on the show!

DELLA. Lovely to be here, George.

VOICE. Tell us about yourself!

DELLA. Well, my name is Della Brady, I love me some buttercream, and I am the proud owner of Della's Sweets in Winston. I make cakes for any occasion. Just name the occasion!

VOICE. Very good, Della!

MACY. I read somewhere all those shows are rigged.

> *Lights return to normal, to the bakery.*

DELLA. *(Firm.)* This one *isn't*.

> *Then:*

You should watch the show! When it comes on! You'll see, / it's –

MACY. Oh, I can't do food TV. It fetishizes an industry that's killing hundreds of thousands of people a year.

Also it makes me hungry.

> **DELLA** *feels shut down. Starts to wonder about Macy's intentions here.*
>
> *But she tries to stay polite. Stick to what she knows.*

DELLA. ...I guess you're not interested in a cake, then.

MACY. Oh. I'm so rude. I'm sorry. You have coffee?

DELLA. I do!

MACY. I'll take a coffee, do you have soy?

DELLA. ...No.

MACY. Black. Thanks.

> **DELLA** *prepares* **MACY***'s coffee, then hands it to her.*

Thanks.

> *She takes a sip. Hides a grimace.*

DELLA. Is it – it's just Maxwell House.

MACY. It is great, it is so great.

> **MACY** *jots down a few more things.* **DELLA** *watches. Unsure what to make of it.*
>
> *She tries so hard to keep being polite.*

DELLA. ...So are you working on a book?

MACY. Sort of. Not really. I mean, that's the dream, but right now, I just do articles.

DELLA. Well that is so neat, have I read any of them?

MACY. I don't know, maybe? *HuffPo, Jezebel, Slate –*

DELLA. *Jezebel?*

MACY. Do you read it?

DELLA. She was not the nicest lady. In the bible. She was a – fallen woman.

MACY. Exactly.

> *Beat.*

DELLA. Well that is just so neat!

> *And she has no more to offer on the subject.*

I like books! They put me right to bed.

> *She stands there, hating her words as they float in the air.*

MACY. Yep! That's what they're there for.

DELLA *forces a kind smile. Busies herself with business.* MACY *tries to drink her coffee. She writes.*

DELLA. I feel like I don't understand what you're writing down, I don't feel like I'm sayin' anything all that profound –

MACY. I don't get much of this in the city. Everybody thinks the exact same thing. So being down here's refreshing.

DELLA. The city?

MACY. New York. I / live –

DELLA. I WENT ONCE, I WENT TO *WICKED*!
    You live there?

MACY. I do!

DELLA. Is your shower in your kitchen?

MACY. I live in Brooklyn.

DELLA. Is that good?

MACY. It means my shower is not in my kitchen.

DELLA. Well, that is so cool.
    You gotta try a piece of my pink lemonade cake. It's my specialty.

MACY. Oh – no thank you –

DELLA. I am not letting some article writer from New York come in here and just leave with the taste of bad coffee in her mouth.

MACY. It's not that / bad –

DELLA. Honey, we both know it is. I gotta get a piece'a cake in there. Come on, now. Open says me.

MACY. Oh – thank you so much, but I don't do gluten.

DELLA. Aw, are you allergic?

MACY. It's just – parameters I set for myself.

DELLA. We went to see Tim's cousin, that's my husband, we went to see his cousin in Boston and I tried a gluten-free cake and it tasted like the back of my mouth after I have a good cry. Now, that is just *wrong*. You poor thing, somebody needs to invent a good kind of cake for you.

MACY. They have. I just don't eat it. It's kind of a slippery slope for me.

DELLA. So you don't –

MACY. I don't eat cake.

DELLA. *(A joke.)* Where do you get your pleasure from?

MACY. Sex, knowledge, Greek yogurt –

DELLA. You need cake.

MACY. Really, no thank you. I'm okay. I have a bar.

> *She reaches into her bag, finds a protein bar.*
>
> *She unwraps it.*
>
> **DELLA** *watches. The bar makes her sad.*

DELLA. What kind is it?

MACY. Peanut butter cookie.

DELLA. That's not a cookie.

> **MACY** *eats her bar, writes.*
>
> **DELLA** *suddenly feels like she must say something intelligent, something amazing, something quotable. And so she selects:*

I read about what's going on with ISIS and I think to myself, if cake were just free for everybody, there would really be a whole lot less problems in the world!

> *Beat.*

MACY. ...So...wait, you're saying –

DELLA. If I could just make every person a cake with their name on it, a lot of problems would be solved.

MACY. ISIS has some eighty thousand members and it's growing. You couldn't possibly make a cake for every member of ISIS.

DELLA. ...It's a silly sorta idea, I know. I just like the essential idea of it, that's all.

> **MACY** *writes. And so* **DELLA** *keeps talking.*

I just think there's still a whole lotta goodness. In the world. We forget that. But it's there. Sometimes I wake up and I say, "Jesus, *you are a magician.*"

MACY. Why?

DELLA. ...For all of the magic I see him working in the world. Every day.

MACY. Yeah, but is it definitely him though?

DELLA. Oh sweetie, I believe it is.

MACY. But it just makes me wonder, though, how can people base their entire belief system on a book that's thousands of years old? And shouldn't we be humble, I mean, epistemologically speaking?

DELLA. ...Yes! We should.

MACY. "The only thing I know is that I know nothing."

DELLA. Is that a – who / said that?

MACY. Socrates.

DELLA. Right. Well. I think I know more than nothing. I feel like I know where I came from.

Why I'm here. Where I'm going. And that's good enough for me.

I'm not a political person.

MACY. Yeah, but, don't you think –

> *She stops. But then she can't help herself. She must say something.*

I mean, you live in this world, and the world is molded by politics, so don't you kinda *have* to be a political person?

DELLA. I just. I just try not to worry about everything. I focus on my cakes. That's my part of this world.

MACY. *(Can't help herself.)* Ambivalence is just as evil as violence.

> **DELLA** *suddenly feels very naked. Exposed. Ashamed.*
>
> *She moves her hands over her body, sweatering herself with her own limbs.*
>
> *At the same time,* **MACY** *suddenly feels self-conscious too.*
>
> *Wonders if she's taken it a step too far.*

DELLA. Will you excuse me? I got a pineapple upside down in the oven back there, I gotta check on it.

MACY. Absolutely.

DELLA. *(Please be gone when I get back.)* It was so nice talking to you.

MACY. You too! And congrats on the cake, ah, competition thing.

DELLA. *(Correcting.) The Big American Bake-Off*.

MACY. Yeah.

> **DELLA** *forces a smile.*
>
> *Goes into the back.*
>
> **MACY** *is alone.*
>
> *Before she even understands what's happening, she leans down to one of the cakes. And she smells it. Smells it deep. She nearly cries. Mother Fuck. It smells so good.*
>
> **JEN** *enters and* **MACY** *jumps back. She was not just smelling a cake, not at all.*
>
> **JEN** *has a large binder marked "Wedding Binder" that she could use as a house if she ever needed to, and a giant bag from Michaels craft store. She has a niceness to her, like she is full of manners and sweet tea.*

Sup, girl.

JEN. I thought you were waiting in the car.

MACY. I had to pee! And I didn't know how long you'd be. You get weird in craft stores.

JEN. No I – do. Is she here?

MACY. She's in the back.

JEN. Did you talk to her?

MACY. Just like, hi, and stuff.

JEN. Did you tell her who you are?

MACY. Who am I?

JEN. Were you weird?

MACY. No. But just so we're clear about who we're dealing with here: she wants to make cake for all of ISIS.

JEN. ...This is why I didn't want y'all talking, first, before I –

MACY. Why do you have an accent all the sudden?

JEN. This is how I talk. LOOK WHAT I GOT, LOOK WHAT I GOT.

MACY. Oh, lord, here we go –

> JEN *hefts the bags onto a table.*
>
> *A glimpse of a little girl who once marched Barbie up a carpet aisle.*
>
> MACY *can't help herself. She is delighted by the girl inside of this woman. Loves her, even. Wants to spend her life next to her.*

JEN. TINY LIGHTS THAT MATCH THE COLORS EXACTLY.

MACY. Okay, there's no need to shout.

JEN. We can put them all up and down the aisle. Line the perimeter. It'll feel like we're floating in stars, like we're made of light, which I think could be our theme!

MACY. I thought our theme was "mother fuckin' loveeeee."

JEN. That's – well yes. But that's – you need like a visual theme that serves as an extension of the love itself. Our love is definitely stars. 'Cause we always have been, and we always will be.

MACY. Our love is definitely thirty thousand dollars that we could spend on something else!

JEN. Could you please stop –

> *They've had this argument 100 times. They're used to it.*

My mom left me the money. For *this.*

MACY. But don't you see how that's –

JEN. Nope, I don't see and I don't *want* to see.

> JEN *avoids.*

>*Spots the cakes. Starts to look at them.*

The cake! Cake cake cake.

MACY. *(A sad huzzah.)* Cake.

JEN. Pink lemonade!! That's the one my mom always got me for my birthday!!

What're we thinking?

MACY. I think the correct question is what're *you* thinking.

JEN. Well what do you like?

MACY. You know I don't / eat cake.

JEN. I know, but on your one day, on your wedding day, obviously you will.

MACY. I will?

JEN. Yes, I am going to shove it in your face and it's going to be adorable.

We could go German chocolate because of the German on your dad's side –

AHHHHHH STRAWBERRY SHORTCAKE!

MACY. Does it really matter?

JEN. EVERYTHING MATTERS.

>*Then:*

I just want it to be perfect. And I know, they say *It's not supposed to be perfect, don't expect it to be perfect,* but *they* are not me and do not have my experience with event planning, and so, I would please like for it to be perfect. RED VELVET CAKE I FORGOT ABOUT RED VELVET CAKE.

>*Her attention is now back on the cakes.*

MACY. Can we pleeeeeeeease just go to the Food Tiger where it's thirty bucks and nobody asks questions?

JEN. It's a Food *Lion*. I want to get it from here.

MACY. Ma'am, can I get your eyes for a second, like your full eyes?

>**JEN** *looks at her fully.*

There's already enough drama doing this here. I'm just asking, why do we have / to –

JEN. She was my mom's best friend.

MACY. Okay –

JEN. There are just things that I – that I feel like should be a certain way, and my mom would've – I know she *wouldn't* have, it wouldn't have been exactly like I – but I just want to do it like we talked about doing it. Even though she's not –

> *She has tears in her eyes.*
>
> **MACY** *takes her hand.*

MACY. Okay. Hey. We'll get it from here.

JEN. Thank you.

> *They kiss.*
>
> *They separate.*
>
> **DELLA** *re-emerges, taking off her oven mitts.*
>
> *She spots* **JEN**.

DELLA. Is that –? No. Jenny Penny?

JEN. Hiiiiiiiii!

DELLA. OH MY GOODNESS! It's you!

JEN. It's me!

> **DELLA** *moves around the counter, comes around to* **JEN**.
>
> *Pulls her into a large, warm, sincere hug.*
>
> **JEN** *puts her arms around* **DELLA**, *too.*
>
> *Their communication is quick, familiar.*

DELLA. Wait, hold on a second, I am mad at you, I am so mad at you right now! You did not return my last email! It was a cat using the toilet, it was so funny!

JEN. Sorry – I think I responded in my mind –

DELLA. And you have not been down to see / me in –

JEN. I just. Work got. And you know my dad moved away.

DELLA. I know, I know.

JEN. I didn't really have a place to come to anymore.

DELLA. You coulda come to me. You can always.

JEN. I know.

DELLA. How's your daddy, how's he like the lake?

JEN. He's good! He got a boat! He named it Debra after Mom.

DELLA. And how's your brother, how's that Kimmy and the kids?

JEN. Good, good, he got transferred, they're in Knoxville? Or Nashville – I can't remember –

DELLA. Well, where you stayin' then?

JEN. With my cousin and his wife – Chip, remember Chip?

DELLA. He's got a *wife*? Got all her teeth?

JEN. Far as I can tell. She's sweet.

DELLA. How're they doin'?

JEN. They're fine!

They're – family.

DELLA. It's a big word, it's empty and it's full at the same time.

JEN. Yeah.

> **DELLA** *has barely noticed that* **MACY** *is still there.* **MACY** *decides to no longer be invisible.*

MACY. Hi. I'm still here.

DELLA. Oh – hello!

JEN. Hi! Sorry!

This is my – this is Macy.

She's with me.

DELLA. Oh!

(To **JEN**.*)* We were chattin' up a storm before –

It is so nice to meet one'a Jenny's friends! You shoulda said / so –

JEN. Jen.

DELLA. Oh. Jen.

JEN. It's not like a big.

Jen, though.

DELLA. Jen!

> DELLA *looks at the two, unsure what to say next.*

JEN. OH! When do you go on the show?

> *(To* MACY.*)* Did I tell you? Della's about to be a contestant on *The / Big American Bake-Off.*

MACY. *Big American Bake-Off*, yep.

DELLA. Six weeks I'm going! I don't even know what I'm gonna wear! I'm takin' myself down to the outlets in Charlotte this weekend, they got a Chico's outlet. But get this, once I get there I am sworn to SECRECY. I can't tell anyone if I won or not 'til they air it!

JEN. Well I'm gonna watch you every week and cheer you on.

DELLA. Thanks, sweetheart, we'll see, we'll see. I'm trying not to think about it! I'm not thinking about it! So, what're you up to this visit?

MACY. Cruising for a wedding cake.

> *This stops* DELLA*'s entire world.*

DELLA. You're getting *married*?!

JEN. I am!

DELLA. AHHHHHHH!!

JEN. I know!

DELLA. I didn't even know you were seeing anybody, why didn't you *tell* me!

JEN. Oh – I just / didn't –

DELLA. Lemme see that diamond, girl, gimme that bling.

> JEN *shows a modest diamond.*

Wait, you didn't want your mama's?

JEN. I didn't want to take it. Just yet.

DELLA. Okay, that's okay. It's a beautiful ring. So, you're doin' it down here?

JEN. Yep!

DELLA. Your mama is dying all over again in her grave right now!! She is watching and she is so stinkin' *mad* she is not here. I am gonna make your cake!

JEN. Oh, that would be amazing, if / you –

DELLA. Now what're your colors?

JEN. Emerald and midnight blue.

DELLA. LIKE THE EARTH ITSELF. I CANNOT IMAGINE PRETTIER. And where's the wedding gonna be?

JEN. Reynolda Gardens.

DELLA. Where your mama and daddy got married! I CAN'T! I CANNOT!

JEN. It makes sense to physically go through the departure on the land where you were born.

It's such a rite of passage, you depart your family, and so –

MACY. She's been reading a lot of bride books.

JEN. I have. It's a thing.

DELLA. It is, it is.

Well, I wanna hear all about him!

> **MACY** *gives* **JEN** *a look: Tell. Her.*
>
> **JEN** *panics. Avoids.*

JEN. Do you still make that carrot cake? My mom used to get it for her birthday, every year –

DELLA. Honey, I have a new and *improved* carrot cake that will make your very dreams beg for cream cheese frosting.

> **DELLA** *gives* **JEN** *a fork of cake.*
>
> **JEN** *eats.*
>
> *She savors.*

Whatcha think, bride?

JEN. Incred/ible.

MACY. Oh, we're both the brides.

> *A beat in which* **JEN** *murders* **MACY** *with her eyes.*

DELLA. ...Beg pardon?

> **MACY** *shoots* **JEN** *a look that is meant to give her a shot of bravery.*

> **JEN** *pushes forward with the truth. Her heart racing.*

JEN. We are both. Are.

DELLA. Oh.

MACY. We both are.

> **DELLA** *realizes what they're saying.*

DELLA. ...Oh!

JEN. Macy's my.

I'm sorry to spring it on you, but – yeah! So.

DELLA. *(Trying.)* Well, congratulations to you two!

JEN. Thank you!

DELLA. When, ah. When is the wedding?

MACY. Six months!

DELLA. Wow! Okay!

MACY. We want to do it in the fall before fall is no longer a thing, which really isn't that far off.

JEN. And I didn't want a super long engagement because I feel like that really dilutes the process. And so we're just kind of throwing it together.

MACY. By which she means she has a wedding binder and multiple spreadsheets.

JEN. I'm really into schedules. And also Sharpies.

MACY. And tabs, you love tabs.

JEN. *Love* tabs.

DELLA. Well.

I think, ah. That I, ah.

October, is it?

JEN. Yup!

> *She senses* **DELLA***'s discomfort. It kills her.*

I know it's late notice –

> **DELLA** *pulls open a drawer, nervously starts to sift through it. Pulls out a messy binder, flips through it.*

I – I shoulda called –

(To **MACY**.*)* She gets a lot of orders –

DELLA. Let me just – I got my own binder, here!

> *She flips through a bit more.* **JEN** *dies, watching her.*

JEN. If you don't – I'm sure you're super busy –

DELLA. You know, you know what, I am so sorry, but you're right, I think I am all backed up, around that time, a lot of fall weddings, it's a favorite time for a lot of people –

JEN. It's okay – I understand –

DELLA. A lot of people like the fall air! Apple cake, hot cider, all of that, jumping into those piles'a leaves though my daddy used to tell me, sometimes bad people hide knives in there so you must always check first.

> *She has no idea why she just said that. And so, she just keeps talking.*

I think that I ah, yes, it looks here like I've got a lot of orders already for October, and it is very important for me not to overcommit myself. I pride myself on quality over quantity. So.

JEN. It's fine, it's so fine, we can / get it somewhere else –

DELLA. It's not – because – it's just I have a lot –

MACY. *(To* **JEN**.*)* We should get going to that next thing that we have to get going to.

> **JEN** *just stands there, frozen.*

Jen?

DELLA. I am so sorry –

JEN. *(Humiliated.)* No, I'm sorry, it's totally / fine, it's.

DELLA. Stop by again and see me, whenever you –

JEN. Definitely!

> **JEN** *and* **MACY** *go.*
>
> **DELLA** *stands there helplessly.*
>
> *Again, stage lights pop on.*

VOICE. Welcome back to *The Big American Bake-Off*!

Each week, contestants will be given a baking challenge. Those who fall short will be asked to leave. Who is up to the task? And who will be left behind?

Della!

What have you done?

DELLA. What?

VOICE. What the hell have you done?

DELLA. I did the right thing? I think.

VOICE. In the oven. What did you *bake*. Tell us what you *baked*.

DELLA. Oh.

This. Right here.

She presents a chocolate cake.

This here is my devil's food.

The trick is to use the Dutch-processed cocoa powder and nothing else. I baked it for twenty-six minutes at 350. Not a minute more or less.

Devil's food gets its name from angel food cake, which is vanilla. Add a little chocolate and you got yourself something sinful.

But do not be deceived. It's full of angel saliva and good deeds.

This cake is not sin. It is a *reward*.

See I think God made butter and sugar as rewards for us, for our good choices, for sticking to what's right no matter how much the world changes.

Because the world's gonna change and we cannot.

Right?

No answer.

Right? Right.

She takes a bite.

The room closes in around her, wet with whipped cream and with her choices.

Her cakes glow as if being judged.

She stares at them. This perfect part of herself.

Scene Two

Della and Tim's bed. 9:00 p.m. Floral and pillow and fluff.

TIM *is lovable. Big gut. Working class.*

They lay next to each other.

TIM *has a comforting hand on* **DELLA***'s breast like it's a cloud he can touch.*

It's not sexual. Maybe it used to be, but it's not anymore.

TIM *flips the channels.*

News, news, sitcom, news, porn.*

The sounds of porn.

They both study it. Unphased. Unaroused.

TIM. Cleaned some condoms out of a septic tank today!

No response from **DELLA.**

The kids flush 'em to get rid of the evidence.
The kid was home. Begged me not to tell his parents. I said, "Secret's safe with me."
Houses all clogged up with secrets and such.

No response from **DELLA.**

Oh! Honey! I wanted to tell ya – I heard this ad on the radio today! "Smell Good Plumbers." A whole plumbing business based on smellin' good. Can you believe it? That is stereotyping! If your plumber does happen to smell, maybe he might do better work or charge a fairer price than a plumber who shows up smellin' like France. How does odor correlate with quality of work?

Beat.

I usually smell pretty good, don't I?

---

*A production license to perform *The Cake* does not include performance usage rights for any sitcoms, news reels, or pornographic videos. Licensees should create their own sound effects or use sound effects in the public domain.

DELLA. Right now, you do not smell amazing.

TIM. Well I pride myself on my appearance. All'a my guys, we tuck our shirts in, we wash our hands. And so I find that offensive. If everybody else is allowed to get offended by this or the other, then I get to be offended, too.

>   **DELLA** *is still lost in space.*

Hey! I am trying to have a cuddle and ask you about your day, Little.

DELLA. You're not asking, you're telling.

TIM. I was getting to the asking part!

DELLA. Go on, have your cuddle.

>   **TIM** *cuddles up to her.*

TIM. I'm gonna miss you when you go.

DELLA. It's just six weeks. Maybe less if I mess up.

TIM. Yeah but when was the last time we were apart for a month?

DELLA. I don't know, before we met?

TIM. Yep. So I can be dramatic if I want to.

>   *Beat.*

You better not get all Hollywood on me.

DELLA. What does that mean?

TIM. All wantin' to eat sushi all the time.

DELLA. You know I can't stand that seaweed stuff.

TIM. Just make sure you come back the same.

>   *This lands on* **DELLA.**
>
>   *She contemplates what he's saying. It does not sit right with her.*
>
>   *He finally clocks that something is wrong.*

...What?

DELLA. Jenny came into the store today.

TIM. Jenny's in town?

DELLA. She is.

TIM. Well we gotta have her over! You can make that cornflake fried chicken!

DELLA. I'll ask her.

TIM. Or is she still pretending she don't eat meat? Last time she was down, remember that? Took her to Little Richard's? I watched that girl eat a plate of just green beans and collards, it was upsetting. Honestly, I got upset. She's getting all corrupted by the liberals up there, sweat yoga, and all'a that.

DELLA. I think she was just experimenting.

TIM. That's how it starts. It starts small with experiments just 'cause everyone else is doing them. Next thing you know, you forget who you are, where you came from.

DELLA. She's getting married!

TIM. That is wonderful news! Who's the lucky guy?

DELLA. The lucky guy is. It is a woman.

TIM. ...What?

DELLA. Don't say "what" when I know you heard me, we are both sittin' right here.

It's a woman, a very beautiful black woman.

Not that I have a problem with that, you know I don't see color.

TIM. I don't care if she's blue with green spots, Little, since when is Jenny – didn't she have that boyfriend in college? That short – he was a nice short fella. He was from, where was he from, he was from India or Indiana –

DELLA. Yeah, she did.

TIM. Well then how is it that she's marryin' a girl?

DELLA. Well I don't know, Tim, I didn't start liking olives 'til just last year, and my whole life before it I thought they were like eyes. But now I cannot get enough.

She was – all lit up. From the inside. They both were.

TIM. Well, good for them. They can take themselves to California.

DELLA. It's legal here, too. They passed a *law*, Tim, where've you been?

TIM. I have been at *work*, payin' my taxes! I got four yards drowning from busted septic tanks, I got a broken Speedrooter and six guys on my payroll with families to feed.

DELLA. They want me to make their wedding cake.

> **TIM** *scoffs*.

What's funny?

TIM. It is unfair'a Jenny to put you in that situation.

DELLA. She's Jen, now.

TIM. Is that a lesbian thing?

DELLA. I think it's just her name.

TIM. Well, you had every right to tell 'em no.

> *Beat.*

DELLA. I didn't tell you I told them no.

TIM. Didn't you?

DELLA. I told 'em I had a full month already.

And I do. I *do* have a full month. I got two christening cakes and I do like to take my time on those, plus Halloween so I do my pumpkins.

I *do* have a lot.

TIM. Sweetie. You don't have to justify your decision to me. I'm on your side, here.

DELLA. You shoulda seen her face. It was the worst face I ever seen.

TIM. We know we can't pick and choose the bible, honey. That's when the edges start to blur.

Fabric starts to fray. We can be sad for her, though. We can love her, still.

DELLA. So I can make her cake?

TIM. That's not what I said.

> **TIM** *kisses* **DELLA**'s *doughy cheek*.

Love ya.

He settles into his pillow.

Turns out the light.

The kiss stays fresh on **DELLA**.

She sits there doing the mental math of marriage. When did they last have sex? She lets this pass.

DELLA. It's not like I've never known a gay person before, I know plenty.

TIM. Who?

DELLA. Well geez, there's the nice boy with the purple hair who makes my frappuccino. There's Robert –

TIM. Who is Robert?

DELLA. Robert! That realtor we used when we tried to sell the house! He was always wearing those bow ties!

TIM. Fifteen years ago. You do not "know" Robert.

DELLA. Yeah. I guess I've just – never known any very *well*. Not on purpose.

> *Then:*

Or, maybe on purpose?

TIM. I'm turnin' in, here –

DELLA. I'm trying to ask you a *question*.

TIM. What's your question?

> *Beat.*

DELLA. I don't know yet.

> *Beat.*

They seem so happy together. The way Jenny smiled – how her – Macy, is her name, how Macy was looking at her –

TIM. Please spare me the details.

DELLA. I am just telling you what I observed.

TIM. And I am telling you I don't wanna think about it.

> *Beat.*

DELLA. Why not?

TIM. Why *not*? Because it's – it's gross.

DELLA. Love is gross?

TIM. That particular / *kind* of –

DELLA. Am *I* gross?

TIM. No!

> DELLA *sits there, feeling gross.*

It's – it's just not natural.

DELLA. Well, neither is confectioner's sugar!

> TIM *rolls back onto his side, fights with his pillow.*

TIM. You're not making that cake.

DELLA. *(Soft.)* I'll make it if I want to.

TIM. What's that?

DELLA. Nothing.

> *A few soft, still moments.* DELLA *digs further into her own brain.*
>
> TIM *falls asleep.*
>
> DELLA *is still troubled. Stays up.*
>
> TIM *starts to softly snore, out like a light, like clockwork.*

Well, I don't wanna think about it, either.

I can't think about it.

> *But she lies there, thinking about it.*

So I won't.

> *Her eyes find* MACY *and* JEN *in their own bed, bodies wrapped around each other.*

...I won't...

> DELLA *turns out the light.*
>
> *Goes to bed, or tries.*
>
> *But her eyes stay focused on the show that is* MACY *and* JEN, *in real life and also in her mind, as she imagines their love.*

JEN *is lost in thought. Troubled. Just as* DELLA
was.

MACY *pulls* JEN *toward her.* JEN *lays her face
on* MACY*'s chest, breathing.*

MACY *gently fidgets with* JEN*'s hair, her ear.*

MACY. That time I drove down through here, in high
school, it was my first time going anywhere south
of Philly. When my mom dropped me off at the bus
that morning, she was like, "Careful down there. It's
different down there."

The more south we got, the billboards started to change.

They were all lit up like beach t-shirts.

"Evolution is a fairy tale for grown-ups."

"'Don't make me come down there.' – God."

Or just, "JESUS!"

JEN. That one's my favorite.

MACY. They were all paid for by churches.

That's when I realized that down here, church is just
another chain store.

JEN. Well, that's a generalization.

MACY. Is it, though?

JEN. *(Diverting.)* At least down *here*, you can have a real
house.

With countertops.

And CLOSETS.

Multiple closets. A whole closet just for winter coats.

MACY. *(Allowing the diversion.)* Wait, so *what's* a closet?

JEN. It's a thing you hang your clothes in.

If we lived here, we could have CLOSETS. We could
have a house with countertops and closets and a
staircase and a big yard with a dogwood tree and a tire
swing and a little creek out back –

MACY. Here? For actual life? Nope.

MACY*'s reaction does not sit well with* JEN.

JEN. You can't even pretend?

MACY. Pretend what?

> *After a few moments,* **JEN** *sits up. Reaches for her clothes.*

Where're you going?

JEN. They made up the couch.

MACY. We just had sex in their house.

JEN. But we're not married yet.

I know it's stupid.

I just don't want to rub it in their faces.

MACY. By sleeping next to me?

JEN. I don't want them to have to think about it. And neither do they. Which is why they made up the couch.

MACY. They won't even notice. They're asleep.

JEN. They'll know, and then Chip'll mention it to my brother or my dad, and it'll just –

MACY. But they know / we –

JEN. Yeah, but. Still.

MACY. You said they were fine with it.

JEN. Yeah, well they are. But that doesn't mean they like it. So I just. I don't want to make them have to think about it.

MACY. Okay so – I think that inviting them to watch us marry each other is making them think about it.

JEN. They're my family and I want them there and that's how I want it!

MACY. Whatttt is happening?

JEN. What?

MACY. Ever since we got down here. You sound like a little kid.

JEN. Well, I never said I was a fully formed human! I never said that!

MACY. Just stay here.

Go down in the morning.

JEN. I already *did*!

She goes to high five **MACY**, *who won't return it.*

MACY. You're not cute.

JEN. You're making this a bigger deal than it is. It's just a formality.

> **JEN** *pulls on her clothes. Grabs an extra pillow to take down with her. Playfully throws it at* **MACY**. **MACY** *does not play back.*

MACY. She's wrong. The Cake lady.

JEN. Della.

MACY. She's wrong.

JEN. She has every right to say no if she's not / comfortable –

MACY. She is wrong.

JEN. She doesn't think she is.

MACY. Look at me. SHE IS WRONG.

> **JEN** *is quiet. Puts her head in her hands.*
>
> *A few moments.*

JEN. I shouldn't've gone there. You shouldn't've seen that.

MACY. *(Softly.)* What'd you think was going to happen?

JEN. I had this whole speech prepared. I had lines. I was going to say them to her.

The last few weeks I kept imagining myself saying it, all calm and confident.

But then I saw her face. And I just. I couldn't.

I feel like such a tiny piece of shit.

MACY. Hey. You are a completely normal-sized piece of shit.

> **JEN** *can't help but smile at this.*

You're not shit. You're hopeful.

JEN. Hope is stupid.

MACY. You're not allowed to say that 'cause I'm pretty sure you're one of the last people on the planet who has any of it. Like, at all.

> **JEN** *is quiet as her hope slowly slips from her.*

MACY. ...You could change her.

JEN. Della? No, thank you.

MACY. But if you don't push her to change then they / never will.

JEN. They?

MACY. All of them.

JEN. I'm not talking about all of them, I am talking about one person, who I love, who I know.

MACY. See, you could start there!

JEN. Why does it have to be me? Why can't it be a very good article or a fictional character?

MACY. It doesn't have the same impact. You know it doesn't.

JEN. Don't make this about your dad, 'cause / it's not the same –

MACY. I'm *not*. It's just frustrating for me to see you compartmentalize yourself like this for no reason.

JEN. *(Soft.)* There's a / reason.

MACY. You couldn't even tell her who I was. I had to.

JEN. Which was my news to share.

MACY. Then you shoulda shared it.

> JEN *burrows into* MACY. MACY *lets it happen.*

I'm just asking – do we really have to do this *here*?

JEN. YES. My mom wanted me to get married here. We talked about it. Her whole last two months. What it would look like, what I would wear, what my dad and I would dance to –

MACY. Baby, that was five years ago. You've changed a / lot since then –

JEN. *Yes.* We have to.

MACY. We do not "have" to do anything, okay? We are shoving ourselves through some narrow / system that was not even designed to support us! I don't need you to be my property. I have no desire to own you.

JEN. I know, I know, "narrow system" –

MACY. Can we just – we could take that money from your mom, we could go to Goa, you've always wanted to go to Goa –

JEN. Mostly because it's fun to say.

The money is for a wedding. And I want a / wedding.

MACY. I know. You always dreamed.

> *Beat.*

JEN. All I ask is that you just try and be respectful of the people / down here.

MACY. ...I don't respect these people.

JEN. ...But I'm one of them.

MACY. No you're not.

JEN. *(Soft.)* I kinda am.

> *Beat.*

I'm gonna go downstairs.

> *Softly,* **JEN** *goes.*
>
> *Frustrated,* **MACY** *throws a pillow after her.*
>
> *She lies back down on the bed. She thinks.*

Scene Three

Della's bakery.

The next afternoon.

DELLA *is constructing a red velvet cake, piling on the delicate layers, lost in thought. Off her game.*

Stage lights.

VOICE. Let's check in with Della!

DELLA. *(Nervous, hopeful.)* Hello, George!

VOICE. Della, you have been in the bottom of the competition for three straight weeks! You have failed *all* of the technical challenges!

How does that feel?

DELLA. I'm a bit discombobulated –

VOICE. And what have you made this week, Della?

DELLA. My red velvet!

VOICE. ...Ah.

DELLA. Is that bad?

VOICE. It's a bit – dated.

DELLA. It's a / classic –

VOICE. Well to guarantee your spot on next week's show, just don't make any mistakes ever!

DELLA. That's the plan! Just makin' good choices over here, that's all!

VOICE. Are you sure? Have you followed the instructions to a T?

DELLA. I have, I have. Every little step. I even sifted my baking soda.

VOICE. Well then. I'm sure things will end gloriously.

I can't wait to get you in my mouth.

DELLA. *(Oh, damn.)* ...Oh –

VOICE. I'm going to lick you up and down, Della, lick the skin specifically between your knee and your belly button, Della, because I want you so bad my parts throb at the thought of you, and then I'm going to put you into my mouth.

DELLA. Oh my word –

Distracted by this image, she sloppily places on a layer and accidentally knocks the cake off the counter. A sad thump of cake on the floor.

She goes to rescue it.

Lights return to normal.

No – no no no –

She picks up the cake layer. Tries to salvage it.

It's messy, but she gets it all back on the cake stand.

She's sweating, nerves throbbing from her mistake. She gets it all back onto the counter. Wipes her brow.

JEN *enters. Humbly. Awkwardly.*

With a bag from Chick-fil-A.

DELLA *pretends like everything is normal and fine.*

So does **JEN.**

Hey there!

JEN. You still open?

DELLA. Closing up, but yeah.

JEN. I brought you some nuggets!

DELLA. You are an angel.

JEN. One honey mustard, double Polynesian sauce.

DELLA. You are the QUEEN OF ALL THE ANGELS.

JEN *hands the bag over.*

DELLA *digs into her nuggets.*

You want one?

Then, realizing:

DELLA. Oh. Sorry.

JEN. What?

DELLA. Isn't there something about Chick-fil-A not supporting, ah –

JEN. I support Chick-fil-A going right into my mouth.

She eats a nugget.

Don't tell Macy.

DELLA. I won't.

They eat.

JEN. So business is good?

DELLA. Good, good, yeah, got me four stars on Yelp, got me my loyal customer base!

Then:

But, ah. Doesn't seem to be enough. Last year I lost money on it, so.

Puts a real strain on us. On Tim. I would let it go, but you know.

JEN. It's your baby.

DELLA. Yeah.

The words hang because they are true.

It is so good to talk to you.

JEN *agrees with a smile.*

JEN. You, too.

DELLA. Where's your –?

JEN. She's at Starbucks. She's got some work to do. She thinks I'm looking at favors. Which is of course my next stop.

DELLA. Are you going to Party City?!

JEN. I am, you wanna come?

> **DELLA** *wants nothing more than to live and die in the wedding favor aisle of Party City with* **JEN**.

But she shouldn't. Not like this. She can't. No.
It wouldn't be right.

DELLA. I should ah. I should get home. To Tim.

JEN. Yeah.

    Beat.

I'm sorry I haven't been down. As much.

DELLA. Oh sweetie, that's alright. You got your life up there.

JEN. I do.

DELLA. A whole other life.

    Beat. She tries:

How, ah. Is your daddy excited about the wedding?

JEN. He's trying to be.

DELLA. And so, ah. How does that work? Do both of your daddies walk both of you down the aisle, together?

JEN. No, ah. Macy and her dad.
They don't – so much – have a relationship. Anymore. She hasn't invited him, yet.
But I mean, would it even be a wedding without somebody mad at somebody?!

DELLA. Honey, it would *not*.

    They share a small laugh that makes them
    each the tiniest bit more comfortable.

She's very...smart! Your. Lady. Is that the right word?

JEN. I call her my person.

DELLA. Your person.

JEN. And she is smart. It's scary sometimes.
But she makes me smarter.

DELLA. Hey, I say you're plenty smart! You won that – you got that academic achievement award your senior year!

JEN. I was good at memorizing things. Not internalizing or dissecting them.
Turns out memorizing is actually not what "smart" is.

DELLA. Stop it.

JEN. When we first started talking – Macy and me – we'd be on the phone, and I'd be online, looking up every other word she said. Writing them down. She's good with words. Especially when she's nervous.

DELLA. And so – how did you two meet?

JEN. Oh, um. That assistant job that I got, at that magazine? When I moved back up after Mom died? Macy responded to an ad to do some freelance articles for it. I did a phone interview with her, and after we hung up, she called back and said, "Can we talk more?" She said my voice made her feel "light." And I said okay because I had never in my life had a better time talking to anyone. So we met up. And we talked more and more, and more. And then we just – kept talking. It was – unexpected. I did not expect it.

      DELLA *just nods, trying to stay normal, polite.*

DELLA. Well. Life is full of surprises!

JEN. It is!

I totally get it. / I don't want you to think that I don't get it.

DELLA. No, I'm sorry that / I –

Hm?

JEN. Why you can't – why you're too / busy –

DELLA. I am so sorry, I looked again, and October is just going to be / impossible –

JEN. Della.

It's okay.

I promise.

     Beat.

DELLA. Okay.

     Beat.

What about that nice boyfriend who came to visit a few times? He was so sweet, he was so sweet to your mama.

JEN. Yeah, she liked him. He was a very nice boyfriend. But something was. Wrong.

DELLA. Well sure, it takes a while to find the right person, but –

JEN. I used to cry after we – when he and I –
Because I didn't want to do it.
And it made me wonder if I was messed up somehow. In that category. Of life.
Which I kinda was, I mean I *am*. Or I was, for a while. Because my mom never. Discussed with me.
I mean, there are some kids whose parents tell them from an early age what exactly sex is and what it is for and why it's special and why it's beautiful and sacred and then there's just the rest of us left drunk out of our minds grabbing at each other's hoo-has in the dark.

DELLA. It's a strange thing we do, but when it happens between two people who love each other, two married people – it can be beautiful. When it happens.

JEN. It wasn't, for me. It wasn't beautiful.

DELLA. That doesn't mean you're "messed up."

　　　　Beat.

JEN. When I was first trying to understand – what it was – I was like thirteen? – I used to think that you go to this – place – to have it. To do it. And you don't want to go but you have to. You get Sent.

DELLA. Sent where?

JEN. To this – place?
And if you're a girl they tie you to a table. Like an operating table. Not tie, bind. Metal handcuffs come up around your limbs and keep you there. And you're naked and cold and you don't want it but you have to.
And then there's this scientist person making sure you're strapped in tight.
Then they leave the room but they're watching through a little window in the door like a dentist taking an X-ray. And you're laying there and the room goes dim.
And there's a metal sound from above you.
And then the boy descends.

DELLA. From the ceiling?

JEN. Yeah.

He's strapped to the ceiling and the ceiling is coming down on top of you. He's being lowered on top of you.

And you're squirming and you don't want it but you're stuck and then the boy is on top of you and he's kissing you and he's touching you –

DELLA *leans in. Turned on.*

And you don't want it but you can't do anything about it. And you don't like it, but you know you are supposed to, because they're watching, and so you pretend. You pretend to like it.

And you look to the window at the scientist and that's when you realize or guess that it's not a scientist, it's God and he winks at you and it happens all over again.

They are both lost in this image.

And that's how it felt for me. For a long time.

But when I met Macy it didn't feel like that anymore.

It just felt right.

DELLA. ...Right.

Beat.

JEN. I know. I know you don't think it's right.

DELLA. What do *you* think?

JEN. ...That I love her.

But I, um. I can't stop wondering how my mom would feel?

DELLA. Sweetie.

JEN. I keep ignoring it but it's a question. I just keep shoving it down.

Beat.

What do you think she would've said?

DELLA. Jen –

JEN. Just tell me. Please.

What she would think.

Beat.

DELLA. I think it would break her heart.

This stabs at JEN. *It kills her.*

JEN. ...Yeah.

Tears come. She fights them.

Suddenly the door dings.

MACY *is there.*

She spots JEN *seconds from tears.*

MACY. Are you okay?

MACY *looks to* DELLA.

JEN. Nothing.

It's fine.

Could I just – I'm just going to use your bathroom for a second.

Losing a battle with a sob, she escapes to the back.

MACY *and* DELLA, *alone.*

MACY. What happened?

DELLA. It is a nice Starbucks! They keep it so clean!

MACY. What did you say to her?

DELLA. Oh, when I was about to get married I cried every time I ate, every time I went to the toilet, every time I saw a rabbit, it's just part'a the process.

MACY. What did you *say* to her?

DELLA. I told her the truth.

MACY. And what truth is that?

DELLA. The only one I know.

MACY *takes a breath. Tries not to engage this. But she can't help herself. Not after seeing Jen so hurt.*

MACY. She's a really good person.

DELLA. I didn't say she / wasn't –

MACY. She's warm and she's giving and she won't ever think of herself first. Sometimes I just want to shake her, *think of yourself, it comes so naturally to everyone else*, but she won't eat until everyone is fed. When I get a cold she makes me garlic tea even though she hates garlic, it makes her gag. When her mom was sick she dropped everything and moved back down here.

DELLA. I know she did.

MACY. She has nightmares she's falling into flames. Because of people like you.

> **DELLA** *tries to stay strong. Stick to the party line.*

DELLA. It is not my job to pass judgment on / you –

MACY. Really? Because I feel kinda judged.

DELLA. I just want what's best for Jenny.

MACY. Jen.

DELLA. Jen.

She has been like a daughter to me.

MACY. But you don't even know her anymore.

DELLA. I know her just fine.

MACY. Do you know what she likes to read, how she takes her coffee, how she likes to fuck?

> *The word stabs at* **DELLA**.

DELLA. Excuse me! I know her *heart*.

MACY. So do I. And I love her. And we wanna spend the rest of our lives together. How is that not what's "best" for her?

DELLA. It's – it's not what God intended –

MACY. Stop saying words an old white man yelled at you.

DELLA. My pastor, he is Filipino, from the Philippines!

MACY. That's not even my point.

DELLA. *(Staying strong.)* It's what I believe.

MACY. So you're not even gonna try and understand where she's coming from?

DELLA. Well, you're not tryin' with me, either.

MACY. It's not the same.

> *Beat.*

DELLA. I know what it's like. To feel different.
When I was young I was – bigger than I shoulda been.
And I got teased for that. And that has hurt at times –

MACY. When I was twelve, I weighed almost two hundred
pounds.
I would get crushes on girls that I couldn't understand
so I'd eat Swiss cake rolls instead.
My mom thought I'd get less shit at a private school
than at public, so she saved up and sent me to the
suburbs. Where I was one of two black kids. Where
they called me "Meatball." Where no one would sit with
me. Where I got a crush on a girl named Margaret and
she kissed me with her tongue in the back of the movie
theater but when her friends found out she wrote
"dyke" on my locker in permanent pen. And when my
dad found out, he threw his bible at my head.
It left a mark on the wall.

> *Beat.*

DELLA. He shouldn't'a done that, sweetie –

MACY. Yeah, well, it's good to know where you stand with
people.

> **DELLA** *is thrown. Tries to find her words again.*

DELLA. *(So gently.)* It's just that the way I see it – and I am
just trying to explain – if God intended everybody to
love on everybody, there would be means – for a man
and a man, to –

MACY. Did you procreate?

DELLA. That's not –

MACY. So you didn't.

DELLA. We tried.
But it didn't.

MACY. So what is YOUR marriage for?

DELLA *sees. She does kind of see. She doesn't know what to say. Thoughts and history swirling, opinions forming.*

MACY. Is it just for sex?

DELLA *gets uncomfortable at the word.*

DELLA. The bible made it / very clear –

MACY. Oh, the bible that has been refuted by scholars?

DELLA. It's God's WORD. I don't know about that.

MACY. Well. You *should* know about it. If you're going to form your belief system on it, you really should.

DELLA. *(Firm.)* It is God's WORD. He says so, in Romans 1:26.

MACY. Okay so, you preach love, but then you go and elect a hateful, misogynistic *baby* –

DELLA. Now, hold on / I didn't –

MACY. Jesus, I am so tired of tolerating this. I am so tired of being nice.

DELLA. This is your nice?

MACY. Why do you hate me?!

She starts to tear up.

Why.

Why.

Why.

DELLA. I – I don't –

MACY. Keep on telling yourself that, but you're a bigot. Is that how you want to be seen?

DELLA. *No.*

MACY. Then Please. Do something about it.

JEN returns from the bathroom.

Walks into this fight.

Both MACY and DELLA try to regain composure.

(To JEN.) Can we go?

JEN. Yeah.

(To DELLA.) I'll see you.

DELLA. See you –

> **JEN** *looks at* **DELLA**, *unsure of what to say.*

> **JEN** *nods. She and* **MACY** *go.*

> **DELLA** *stands alone, feeling like the worst person in the history of the world, including all of the fallen women of the bible.*

> *Again, stage lights pop on.*

> **DELLA** *is suddenly self-conscious. She swallows, fixes her hair.*

VOICE. Let's check in with our contestants! Welcome back, Della!

> *Beat.*

I said welcome back, Della!

DELLA. A – a pleasure to be here, George.

VOICE. One question before you get baking, Della.

Are you a bigot?

DELLA. No!

VOICE. Are you surrrrrreeeeee?

DELLA. Wait – what's the definition again?

VOICE. One more question, Della, this husband of yours: when is the last time he fucked you?

> **DELLA** *is stunned. Does not know how to respond.*

Has he fucked you recently, at all?

DELLA. I don't see how that's / relevant –

VOICE. WELCOME TO THE SHOW, BIGOT!

DELLA. I / don't –

VOICE. BAKE, YOU UNDESIRABLE BITCH.

DELLA. I'M TRYING TO –

VOICE. THOU SHALT BAKE.

> *Silence.*
> *Lights throb.*
> **DELLA** *is shaken.*
> *She starts to remove all of her clothes.*

Scene Four

The bakery. Late that night.

DELLA *stands in dim light.*

She is partially naked, with frosting on her secret parts.

She feels the air on her skin.

She isn't sure what to do with her body.

She leans against the counter.

She stands straight up.

She leans again.

TIM *enters, in a rush.*

TIM. Which pipe is it, what burst?

He doesn't see her at first.

DELLA *flips on a small and soft light.*

TIM *jumps when he sees her. The sight of his naked wife – covered in frosting or otherwise – is shocking to him. He hasn't seen it in quite some time. He is instantly ashamed, uncomfortable. He does not know how to act.*

What –?

DELLA. Hello, mister.

TIM. Which pipe burst, you said a pipe burst –

DELLA. I'm naked.

TIM. I see that.

But which / pipe –

DELLA. NO PIPE, THERE IS NO PIPE, TIM.

TIM. What's all over you?

DELLA. Leftover buttercream. It's melting.

You should take your clothes off, too.

TIM *isn't sure how to handle himself. He's embarrassed in a soft sort of way, like he can't find his pajama pants.*

TIM. I – I don't think so, Little –

DELLA. Why not?

TIM. Because we're in public!

DELLA. Shades're down. Door locked behind you.

TIM. We haven't even had dinner yet!

DELLA. I got your dinner right here.

C'mere.

Pretend I'm a cookie. Fresh outta the oven.

TIM. Cookies don't have frosting on them.

DELLA. *(Sweetly.)* This one does.

TIM. Okay – Should I –?

DELLA. I want you to lick it off, Tim. Geez Louise.

> **TIM** *laughs. He is so uncomfortable.*

TIM. I, uh – I don't know –

DELLA. Could you just try?

Please? You love my buttercream!

> *Hesitantly, he goes toward her.*
>
> *Takes a knee.*
>
> *Tries to position himself so that he might lick it off of her.*
>
> *Tries to do so.*

TIM. Oh geez, it got – it went up my nose –

DELLA. Oh – sorry –

TIM. *(Laughing again.)* I don't know about this.

DELLA. Please, just try!

TIM. *(Embarrassed, flustered.)* I did and I don't LIKE it.

DELLA. We are man and woman. Husband and wife. We are married to each other.

TIM. I didn't say we weren't.

Now, put your clothes back on, I had a long day.

DELLA. But –

TIM. Right NOW.

> *His intensity shames her even more.*

*She reaches for her dress. Sadly pulls it over
her head.*

DELLA. Why don't you want to make love to me anymore?

TIM. I – don't – not *want* –

DELLA. Is it because it didn't work? Because we / didn't –

TIM. It's just – it's been so long –

DELLA. And I am trying to change that.

TIM. Is there – are we gonna thaw that lasagna / for dinner?

DELLA. Screw your lasagna, I am your wife!

TIM. What's goin' on here?

Beat.

DELLA. What if I told you one night I snuck downstairs
'cause I couldn't sleep and I ate a whole broken bundt
cake and I watched *The Birdcage* and I liked it?

TIM. Well that'd be / fine.

DELLA. What if I told you I didn't vote for that man. I didn't.
I know you told me to but I didn't.

I stole one'a those stickers off the table and I went to
Baskin-Robbins, instead.

TIM. Okay –?

DELLA. *(Gaining heat.)* What if I told you that once there
was Sarah.

She was my roommate in college.

You forget that, you forget that I went to college but
I did. She was a dancer and her dresses hung on her
body like they were made for her and she walked like a
cartoon princess, and her lips moved around her teeth
like little flower petals and she laughed at my jokes.
And one night I wanted to touch her body. So I reached
out, and I did. Just for a second.

I don't think I'm that way but I had that feeling once
and it took over my whole self. But I was too scared to
feel it. So I pushed it away.

And that happens. A lot. I feel things that I – can't
always explain. And so I push them away.

TIM. What things?

DELLA. I went back through all the verses. When He speaks of Sodom and he speaks of Gomorrah –

TIM. Are we goin' there right now?

DELLA. I feel as if he's not speaking directly of this world. It might be more like a metaphor.

Maybe there's parts of the way things are – that don't work anymore. Did you ever think that?

TIM. C'mon. We can talk about this over dinner.

DELLA. NO. Lemme talk. I wanna keep talkin'. All through my life, every now and again, I'll just be standing somewhere or doing something, like in line at the store or the bank or wherever I am, and suddenly, I'll feel naked. I become aware of my own body, of every inch of it, and I'll feel – ashamed of it. Like I am Sin itself. I think what I might be feeling is the very nudity of Eve. And how she felt when she realized she was not wearing any clothes. She'd been living her life one way, heck, no difference to her. They paint her with leaves over her privates, but chances are, she ran around with all of her business out, naming all of the animals, doing whatever it is that she did. But all the sudden, it felt wrong. And I think she passed that feeling down to me. It's my inheritance. It's *shame*. It makes me not reach for the fruit on my own, Tim. It makes me believe whatever you tell me to, and I don't know if I want that, anymore.

TIM. I don't tell you what to do.

DELLA. You do. And I let you. That's the worst part. I prayed and prayed for a child. You told me to move on. And I did. I *did*. And I thanked God 'cause I still had *you*. But then you just kept on telling me what to do!

TIM. I – I am your husband, and – it is my duty to –

DELLA. That's true. And I am your wife. And we stood in church and we told Jesus and our parents and some cousins and friends that we were going to stand by each other. But well. I have to say that I don't think you

have stood by me because you have not touched me in
that way in I don't even know how long!

And so instead, I make you lemon bars.

And I bring you Snickers bars.

And you get me Russell Stovers for Christmas.

And I make donuts from scratch.

And we stop by Krispy Kreme.

And you bring home eggnog ice cream.

And we share an elephant ear.

And you haven't kissed me with your tongue in ten
years.

And I feel that.

And I think I want that back.

A softness. In here. I want it. So bad.

And I don't think I'm wrong for wanting that.

>   *Beat.*

TIM. It's not that I –

When the doctor told me that I was not, ah. Able to. To
give you. Us. A child.

That was hard.

It's hard for a man.

For a man, it's hard.

When he's not, ah.

DELLA. It doesn't make you any less of a / man –

TIM. But still, I was not – doin' what a man should be doin'.
And I guess it made the, ah, the urge. Go away.

DELLA. It's gone?

TIM. I don't know. It's not your fault.

Just don't have it right now.

DELLA. I could help you find it!

TIM. Not like this.

DELLA. I wanna feel love –

TIM. Like Jenny and her whatever she is?

DELLA. They *do* love each other. / I saw it myself.

TIM. And so now all the sudden, what, you think I don't love *you*?!

DELLA. No, I know you do, it's / not that –

TIM. *(Plowing over her.)* Is there supper at home or do I need to stop?

DELLA. Tots and a pot pie in the freezer.

TIM. Do I need to / pre-heat the oven?

DELLA. 350, ten minutes.

> **TIM** *nods.*
>
> *He goes to the door.*
>
> *He hesitates.*
>
> *Looks at her, feeling terrible, wanting to say something. But she, also, has nothing to say.*

TIM. See you at home.

> *He goes.*
>
> **DELLA**, *alone. A fallen woman on the floor.*

Scene Five

>JEN, *again in the guest room.*
>
>*She is reading something on her phone. It infuriates her.*
>
>MACY *enters. Watches her. Misreads her mood. Thinks she just needs to be cheered up.*

MACY. What can I do?

>You wanna look at your Pinterest page?
>
>Wanna look at veils?

JEN. What is this?

>JEN *shows* MACY *her phone.*
>
>MACY *looks. Her article. Fuck.*

When did you write this?

MACY. Did somebody –

JEN. Yes, somebody posted it, everybody's posting it.

>Did you think I wasn't going to see it?

MACY. I wanted to get it out there, and then I was going / to –

JEN. You have to take it down.

MACY. Anthony loves it.

JEN. Anthony can go fuck himself.

MACY. He asked me to keep eyes out for stories while / I was down here!

JEN. Della is not a *story*. She's my family. You shoulda talked to me first.

MACY. I didn't use her name!

JEN. It's so obvious it's her! Somebody already figured it out in the freakin' comments!

MACY. Well, that's not my fault.

JEN. ...Why would you write this?

MACY. Because I want you to see what she is doing to / you –

JEN. She's just – she's just trying to do what she thinks is *right*.

MACY. Why're you defending her?!

JEN. I don't expect you to get it. It's always been different for you.

MACY. Different how?

JEN. Your mom is a therapist. She buys you weed. Your parents were never even married. Ten years old, you were taking the city bus to school reading *LOLITA*. I thought Lolita was a chapstick color. And we live in Brooklyn! Everyone is a lesbian! We are in a young adult book club *just* for lesbians! There are so many of you / that there is a whole club just for lesbians who JUST enjoy young adult fiction from the late 1980s!

MACY. So many of *us*.

JEN. I feel – torn in half, up there. All the time. There's Hare Krishna and vagina piercings and there's almond butter / and there's global warming and Kickstarters and those little fucking seaweed snacks that taste like the insides of a fish.

MACY. Wait, what's wrong with almond butter?

JEN. And I take it all in because I'm supposed to, because that's where I live and also my mother raised me to be agreeable. And the parties are easier if when people talk shit about people down here, I just nod and say "totally" but my skin starts to burn so in my head, I go away.

I just go away. I go back to my parents' dining room and I listen to them lament just what is wrong with this world, and there is this little part of me who agrees – No matter how much I learn, no matter how many planetariums I go to, how much Richard Dawkins I read – it's still in there. Everything my parents –

Beat.

It was a good part of my life. For so long.

MACY. ...You were raised with those beliefs. And so you get nostalgic. But nostalgia is not a belief system.

JEN. It's not nostalgia. Every time someone says that God doesn't exist a little something inside of me burns – it goes DING. But with fire. I'm of two different minds. All the time.

MACY. I know, and I'm of a HUNDRED! I'm black and I'm agnostic AND I'm a woman AND I'm queer. I'm in a world that is not designed for me. Nothing ever fits. Except *you*.

>   *Then:*

You know why I had to write that.

>   *She lets her desperate plea hang there, hoping it got through to* **JEN**.

JEN. I'm just. I'm still figuring some stuff out.

>   *They both breathe.*

>   *A few heavy moments of indecision, of the future or lack thereof.*

MACY. Remember the letters your mom used to write you when you first moved away, after college? You had a whole box full of them. That red fruit box. Some of them weren't even opened.

JEN. *(Small, sad.)* It's a Shari's Berries box. From some chocolate-covered strawberries she sent me 'cause I was having a bad week at work.

MACY. There was one letter that she wrote when she found out you were living with – the short dude –

JEN. Nathaniel.

MACY. She said that if you were "intimate" with him before marrying him that no man was going to respect you ever again. That if you didn't "change your ways," you were gonna die alone, in Hell.

JEN. In so many words. Yeah.

>   But she meant well. She was just trying to / protect me –

MACY. That's – NO. Parents are supposed to love their children *unconditionally*.

JEN. She *did*.

MACY. *(Hard truth.)* All she gave you is a shame so deep you can't even stand the sound of your own voice.

JEN. That's not *true*.

MACY. Does it ding when you kiss me?

> **JEN** *can't respond.*

Does it?

JEN. ...Not *every* time, but –

> *A horrible confession. The last straw.*
>
> *Spinning,* **MACY** *gathers her things. Throws them into her bag.*

What're you doing?

MACY. I gotta go.

> *She heads to the door.*

This is all maybe stuff you maybe should have "figured out" before you begged me to marry you and finally I said okay, even though my whole life I have pushed that shit far away, but then I started to dream about it, on my own.

JEN. What'd you dream?

MACY. Us. Walking towards each other.

> **MACY** *takes her bag. Goes.*
>
> **JEN** *sits alone with the truth.*
>
> *She is one of them. But she isn't. But she is. But she isn't. But she isn't.*
>
> *But she is.*

Scene Six

Della's bakery, the next day.

DELLA *ices a cake, more determined than ever.*

Next to the cake, a sack of coconut flour, a container of almond milk, some Tofutti.

The cake is rabbit-food brown. It looks mealy. It is an affront to cake.

Stage lights pop on.

VOICE. Welcome back to *The Big American Bake-Off*!

DELLA. *(More anxious than ever.)* Hello, no time to talk, George –

VOICE. For this week's technical challenge, we have a doozy! Bakers, your challenge was to bake a confection of some sort with no dairy, sugar or gluten. I repeat: a baked good with no gluten, sugar or dairy. It must contain NONE of those ingredients, be flawless and delicious *and* morally sound.

DELLA. How do you expect me to make an icing that'll hold with no butter?!

VOICE. Five minutes left, you dirty trollop!

DELLA. You have lost your MINDS!

VOICE. FOUR MINUTES LEFT.

DELLA. I – I'm doing my best here, but I can't –

A layer of the cake starts to slide off.

VOICE. THIS IS YOUR LAST CHANCE!

DELLA. If – if you would just lemme do it *my* way –

VOICE. JUST THIS ONE LIFE, AND THEN IT'S OFF TO ETERNITY!
TWO SECONDS LEFT!

DELLA. That can't be true –

VOICE. TIME'S UP.

DELLA *struggles to finish.*

The ding of an oven.

Lights switch to normal.

Her phone is ringing.

She answers.

DELLA. Hello?

This is she.

She listens. Lights up.

Well hey, I am so looking forward to seeing you soon, I – Sure, I got a minute to talk!

Her face morphs. She is thrown. Confused.

I don't understand. Disqualified why?

...What? What article?

No, I did not see that, no.

She gets flustered. Embarrassed.

I – I didn't say I wouldn't make their cake, I said I was *busy*, I –

She listens.

Well either way, I would say that's got nothing to do with my cakes. They're not – those are separate issues, so I don't see why I –

She listens. Starts to lose her cool. Tears come.

I see – I see –

She listens.

Thank you for the opportunity.

I gotta go now.

I'll talk to you later. Bye bye.

She hangs up. Stunned. Crushed.

JEN *enters with purpose. She looks like she's been up all night. Because she has.*

DELLA *faces* **JEN**, *unsure what to say to her.*

JEN. I used to have nightmares I said *goddamn* in front of my mom and it made her skin melt off her face. That's how scared I was. Of a WORD. She's been gone almost five years and I'm still terrified of disappointing her. That's on *me*.

DELLA. Jen / I –

JEN. Macy's the only person I ever loved. I tried not to love her, but I *do*. She is beautiful and she's wonderful and she's strong. I can never turn my brain off on my own, but she puts her arm over my chest and I sink. Right into sleep. And we have a cat. Cat Stevens. We all get under my great-grandma's blanket and we watch old episodes of *Dr. Quinn, Medicine Woman*. We're a *family*. And I pushed her away because I am so ripped in two. I am straddling two worlds so far I got a tear in me from my cunt up to my eyes. Yeah, I just said cunt. It's a word that I've always been scared to say. I'm SO SICK of being scared.

DELLA. *(Heart breaking.)* Jenny –

　　　Fuck.

Jen –

I would love more than anything, truly anything in this world, to make your cake / but –

JEN. I don't need you to make me a cake. I need you to *love me*.

DELLA. I do love you.

So much that this has been killing me.

So I have really been searching through my heart.

But I just. I *can't* support. What you're doing. I am so sorry to say that.

JEN. I tried not to love her. But I do. I love her so much, I love her –

DELLA. I know, sweetie. But still.

It just – does not sit right with me.

　　　Beat.

JEN. Well then I don't know if I can have you in my life anymore.

DELLA. Oh, no, sweetie – please –

JEN. No, I think that's how it's gotta be right now.

> **DELLA** *closes her eyes. Lets it sting.*

DELLA. I am very sorry to hear that.

JEN. Me too.

> *Neither is sure what to do.*
>
> *They want to hug, but they both know they can't. What's left is the shivering impulse to do so, and the cold lack of it.*

...Bye, Della.

DELLA. Bye, sweetheart. Best of luck, with your –

> **DELLA** *watches* **JEN** *go.*

Jen, I love –

> *But* **JEN** *is gone.*
>
> **DELLA** *stands alone.*
>
> *Alone, alone. The breath knocked out of her.*
>
> *She unclips her fake hair.*
>
> *We now see that she has only a third of the hair she wants us to think she has.*
>
> *She throws her fake hair in the trash.*

Scene Seven

Della and Tim's bedroom.

It's late. The room is dark. We can only make out the shape of **TIM** *lying on the bed.*

DELLA *enters, weary.*

She sits on the edge of the bed. She is still. Very still.

She breathes into her devastation.

TIM. Hey there, Little.

> **DELLA** *breathes in, holding back a sob.*

What's wrong?

DELLA. Jenny doesn't want me in her life anymore.

The show doesn't want me anymore.

TIM. What?

DELLA. "Disqualified."

> **TIM** *processes everything she's just said. Feels terrible for her.*

TIM. *(Soft, trying.)* Well *I* want / you –

DELLA. *(Not hearing him.)* I – I am tryin' – I am open to change, I just – I can't do it overnight, I got a brain and a heart at war –

TIM. How 'bout you turn on the light and maybe I can cheer you up.

DELLA. I just – I can't move so fast, I need a minute to sort it all out!

TIM. LITTLE.

DELLA. What?

TIM. Turn on the *light*.

DELLA. Geez Louise, okay –

> *She goes to the light. Turns it on.*
>
> **TIM** *lies on the bed, naked as God made him, with some food-type item covering his...*

DELLA *is shocked.*

What in the –?

What is that?

TIM. It's mashed potatas. I couldn't find any whipped cream.

DELLA. The instant kind?! I hope you let 'em cool first!

TIM. 'Course I did, I still got *some* sense!

> **DELLA** *starts to laugh.*
>
> *It quickly turns to tears.*

Hey, what is this, now?

DELLA. I just – I can't believe you did this –

TIM. I thought I could. Try. That's all I can do.

DELLA. Thank you. Thank you, Tim.

> **TIM** *moves himself next to her. It might take a few moments.*
>
> *It makes her laugh.*
>
> *He takes her hand. Holds it in his.*
>
> *And he kisses her. It's a long kiss. It's not perfect, but he's trying.*

TIM. Now what?

DELLA. You are going to make love to me all night like a movie star.

> *Something stirs within* **TIM**. *Something he never knew he missed. The beauty of being told what to do. Of not being in charge, just for a moment.*

TIM. *(Stunned, but giving in.)* ...Okay.

DELLA. ...With a British accent.

TIM. *(Trying, badly.)* Right then, my lady.

> **DELLA** *laughs, loving this. They fall back into each other's arms.*

DELLA. Oh, and Tim? I love you.

TIM. I love you, too.

DELLA. That's right.

> *She breathes deep into the part of herself she has just reclaimed.*

This warms **DELLA**. *It's one of the best things she's ever heard.*

DELLA. Where is she?

MACY. She's back at the Gardens in a Disney movie of her own making. Dancing with her dad. I snuck away.

DELLA. Did, ah. Did your father make it down?

MACY. He did not.

DELLA. That is a shame.

> *Beat.*

...Well, how'd the cake turn out?

MACY. I haven't tried it. We didn't do the smush it in each other's faces thing, I had to draw a line somewhere.

DELLA. It's a pretty cake, if I do say so myself.
I did the pink lemonade for Jen, and the carrot cake on top for her mama.

> *Beat.*

Well.
Looks like everything turned out beautifully.

MACY. It really did.

> *Beat.*

It almost didn't. Turn out. *We* almost didn't.

> *Beat.*

But she told me what she said to you. And I was proud of her.
But then she spent the next month crying herself to sleep.
She can't *not* love.
Which is *very* annoying. But it's also why I love her.

> *Beat.*

DELLA. Love's always harder.

MACY. Yeah.

DELLA. *(Remembering.)* ..."Love is patient, love is kind. It does not envy, it does not boast, it is not proud."

MACY. What's that / from?

DELLA. First Corinthians.

> *Beat.*

MACY. I'm sorry about what happened with the show. The Big US, ah –

DELLA. *Big American / Bake-Off.*

MACY. Bake-Off, yeah.

DELLA. It wasn't all bad. Gettin' disqualified made my business go *up. Decision Magazine* ran an ad. It's Billy Graham's magazine. It's called *Decision.* You probably haven't read it.

MACY. I have not.

DELLA. "Rallyin' around me," they said. And that felt nice because.
Because I read some. Very hateful things. About myself.
Tim told me not to google myself.
But I did.
I did.

> *Beat.*

MACY. I have to say so. When things are wrong.

DELLA. When they seem wrong to you.

MACY. When they *are* wrong.

> **DELLA** *eats a piece of the cake.*

DELLA. Oh, that is *good.* I am *good.*

> **DELLA** *eats.*
>
> **MACY** *watches.*
>
> **DELLA** *can sense her watching.*

I guess I thought maybe – I was going to do something great with my life. I never ended up bein' a mom. All'a that. And so, I thought that maybe being on that show was going to be my great thing.

MACY. *(The cake.)* Maybe this is your great thing.

DELLA. What, the cake?

MACY *nods.*

How would you know?

DELLA *takes a forkful. Holds it out to* **MACY.**

MACY *takes a look at the cake. It looks beautiful. But she can't let it in.*

MACY. I – I never let myself –

DELLA. I know, sweetie.

MACY *can no longer stop herself. Fuck it.*

She picks up the fork. Takes a bite.

It is so good.

She looks like she might cry.

It's as if her heart and brain have been pushed open. Filled with sugar and cream and air and love.

MACY. Oh my *God* –

DELLA. Yessir. He made it for ya.

MACY. Oh my God –

MACY *takes another bite. Tears come. It's joyful and pure. She eats more.*

DELLA *watches* **MACY** *eat. It makes her happy.*

DELLA. Maybe you're right. Maybe after all the years, this will have been it.

End of Play

Note: This is the end of the play part of the play. Ideally, upon exiting the theater, the audience is surprised with an actual cake waiting for them. The wonderfully terrible grocery store cake that you never let yourself eat. Ideally, everyone then stands around together, eating cake.